The Pride Street Crew
11
A Thousand Reasons

Mike Wilson

Published in association with
The Basic Skills Agency

Hodder & Stoughton

A MEMBER OF THE HODDER

Acknowledgements
Cover: Jim Eldridge
Illustrations: Jim Eldridge

Orders; please contact Bookpoint Ltd, 39 Milton Park, Abingdon, Oxon OX14
4TD. Telephone: (44) 01235 400414, Fax: (44) 01235 400454. Lines are open
from 9.00–6.00, Monday to Saturday, with a 24 hour message answering service.
Email address: orders@bookpoint.co.uk

British Library Cataloguing in Publication Data
A catalogue record for this title is available from the British Library

ISBN 0 340 77634 X

First published 2000
Impression number   10 9 8 7 6 5 4 3 2 1
Year   2005 2004 2003 2002 2001 2000

Copyright © 2000 Mike Wilson

Typeset by GreenGate Publishing Services, Tonbridge, Kent.
Printed in Great Britain for Hodder and Stoughton Educational, a division of
Hodder Headline Plc, 338 Euston Road, London NW1 3BH, by Atheneum
Press, Gateshead, Tyne & Wear

JOHN / BONE

WESLEY / TALL

LUKE / SKY

SIMON / CUSTARD

CARL / SPOT

'Hey! Give that back!'
Custard shouts.
I run to the door
with his English work book
in my hand.

'Luke, it's not funny,' he says.
'Just give it back here. Now.'

I'm not giving it back.
Not yet.

We've got a test in English next week.
I want a look in Custard's work book.
Custard is good at English
and I'm not.

I go out of Room 6,
and start down the corridor.
I hear his chair fall over,
as Custard comes after me.
I open the book as I start to run.

Then I stop.

On the last pages,
Custard has done some writing.
It's the same thing,
over and over:

> *I must keep my bedroom tidy.*
> *I must keep my bedroom tidy.*
> *I must keep my bedroom tidy.*

About a hundred times.

On the next few pages,
about a hundred times:

> *I must do more homework.*
> *I must do more homework.*
> *I must do more homework.*
> *I must do more homework.*

Custard catches up with me,
and grabs the work book.
He shuts it and puts his arms round it.

I ask him:
'Who made you do this, Simon?
Was it Specky? Or Winker Watson?
Or Mrs Savage?'

'Don't tell anyone,' says Custard.

'It wasn't a teacher, was it?' I ask him.

'Just don't tell anyone, Luke,' he says.
'Please.'

Then I start to think back.

It was a few years ago.
Mr Dodds – Custard's dad –
came in to school.
He came in
to have a word with Mr Baxter,
the sports teacher.

'It's about my Simon,' said Mr Dodds.

'Oh yes,' said Mr Baxter. 'Nice lad.'

'I'd like you to put him
in the school football team.'

Mr Baxter frowned.

'The thing is …' Mr Dodds went on.
'my Simon is not very confident.
He needs a lot of pushing.
If you don't push him,
he doesn't do anything.

Put him in the football team.
It will be good for him.
He'll get more confident.
It will do him good.'

Mr Baxter said:

'Simon is not in the team.
He's not that good at football.
Other boys are better.
I'm sorry, but …
it's that simple.'

'Don't expect too much of the lad,'
Mr Baxter went on.

But Mr Dodds had walked away.

Custard told me all about it.

'I didn't even want to be in the football team,'
he said. 'I know I'm not that good.'

I tried to help:
'You're not bad.

You're better than Girl
and you're better than Sticky.
You're better than Tool ...'

'I wanted to play chess for the school.'
Custard went on:
'Dad says chess is better than football.
Chess is for clever people.'

'Nobody plays chess any more.
Not like when Dad was at school ...'

I don't say anything.
I'm thinking about Red Nose Day.

A few months ago,
we had a Red Nose Day at school.
We all did stupid things,
and made money for charity.

Some mums and dads came.
They joined in the fun.
It was all for charity.

But not Custard's dad.
He didn't join in the fun.

There was a 3-legged race.
Custard and I were tied together.

Before the start,
Mr Dodds came over to talk to us.

'Now, Simon,' he said.
'You can win this, if you try hard.
I want you to keep on your feet,
and keep a steady pace.'

'Don't worry,' he went on.
'I will be right here,
next to you,
telling you what to do.'

Custard went red,
and looked at his feet.

'*Stand up straight*!' his dad hissed.
'DON'T look at your bloody feet all the time!'

Poor Custard.

We didn't win, of course
and the look on his dad's face ...

Sometimes on Saturdays
I'm in the market,
working for my uncle.
I stack the fruit and veg.
I pack the boxes away.

Today Uncle Ray has another job for me.

'Pop to the library for me, Luke,' he says.
'I've got to take this Talking Book back.'

I run to the library,
and drop off the tapes.

Then I see them.

There, in the library,
on a Saturday.

Mr Dodds is sitting at a table,
reading the paper.
Next to him is Custard.

He's got his school books out,
all over the table.

Mr Dodds looks at his watch.
He turns the page.

Custard goes on working.

I talked to Custard about it at school.

It's extra homework,' he said.
'My dad says
I need to do as much as I can.
He sits with me,
to make sure I work hard
and I can ask him things.'

'You can do too much ...' I said.

'GCSEs are coming up ...' said Custard.

'Yes,' I said. 'Next year!'

He just goes on talking:
'... Dad says he'll pay me £100
for each grade A that I get.'

Custard looked wild.
He had dark blue rings under his eyes.

'So I've got to work hard.
I've got to do it.
For him.'

Custard was doing ten GCSEs.
That made £1,000
if he got them all.

That's a lot of pressure for a kid.
It's a thousand reasons
for working day and night,
and getting no sleep.

It's a thousand reasons
for going crazy with stress
at the age of 16.

I wanted to tap his head,
and shout 'Hello?
Is there anybody home?
Will the real Simon Dodds come out
and talk sense to me?'

But I didn't.
I didn't stop him.
I just let him get on with it.

That's why I blame myself
for what he did later.

After that,
I didn't see Simon much for six months.
I had one or two problems of my own.
Problems with me and Lizzy.
Problems with Tamsin Taylor
and problems with Mark Paine.

Just normal problems.

Then one day my mum said:
'Did you hear about Simon Dodds?
He used to be your pal, didn't he?
They had to rush him to hospital
on Sunday ...'

I went cold.

I knew what Custard had done
and I knew why.

I went to see him in hospital.
Me and the Pride Street Crew.

I took him a football mag to look at.
He had his school books open
all over the bed.
Homework.

We didn't know what to say.
He had a tube in his arm,
and a tube up his nose.
He didn't say much.
After a few minutes,
we left.

I don't know if Simon was sad
or just stupid
for doing what he did.

He had a thousand reasons
to be stressed out.
A thousand reasons
to want to kill himself.
So maybe he was just sad.

Maybe the stupid one was his dad
for pushing him so hard.

Or maybe his mum was the stupid one
for leaving her sleeping pills
where he'd find them.

Or maybe the Crew,
his friends, let him down.

I don't know.

I don't know who's to blame.
I'm just glad he's going to be OK.

LIVEWIRE YOUTH FICTION

If you have enjoyed reading about the Pride Street Crew, you may be interested in other books in the series.

It's Not The Winning
Carrot Rap
You Can't Be A Kid For Ever
She Likes Me
No Turning Back
Child's Play
Say it to my Face
Damp Dog
Who Do You Love?
Let's Go Shopping
Make A Splash!
Now I Know How It Feels
You're Never Alone With A Phone